Humpty Dumpty's Great Fall

First published in 2009
by Wayland

This paperback edition published in 2010

Wayland
338 Euston Road
London NW1 3BH

Wayland Australia
Level 17/207 Kent Street
Sydney, NSW 2000

Series Editor: Louise John
Editor: Katie Powell
Cover design: Paul Cherrill
Design: D.R.ink
Consultant: Shirley Bickler

A CIP catalogue record for this book is available from the British Library.

ISBN 9780750256032 (hbk)
ISBN 9780750258142 (pbk)

Printed in China

Wayland is a division of Hachette Children's Books,
an Hachette Livre UK company
www.hachettelivre.co.uk

Humpty Dumpty's Great Fall

Written by Alan Durant
Illustrated by Leah-Ellen Heming

WAYLAND

Humpty Dumpty was a big bad egg.
He called himself the king of Eggtown.
But Humpty wanted to be the king
of the world outside Eggtown, too.

Outside Eggtown there was a great high hill with a tall, crumbly castle wall, which had a ladder beside it. Next to the wall was a deep well.

Each morning, children came to fetch water from the well. They raced to see who could get to the top of the hill first.

The winner climbed up the ladder and
stood on the wall, chanting, "I'm the
king of the castle, get down you
dirty rascal!"

Humpty Dumpty watched and he listened. "I'm going to be the king of the castle," he said to himself.

Early one morning, Humpty Dumpty waddled his way up the hill. He climbed up the ladder and sat on the wall.

Two dicky birds flew down.
"Hello," they tweeted. "We're
Peter and Paul. Who are you?"

"I'm the king of the castle," said
Humpty, and he waved his arms. "Get
down, you dirty rascals!" he cried and
he frightened the birds away. "Ha! Ha!
Ha!" laughed bad old Humpty Dumpty.

A pussy cat jumped onto the wall.
"Miaow," said the cat. "Who are you?"
"I'm the king of the castle," said
Humpty. "Get down, you dirty rascal!"

Humpty Dumpty picked up the
pussy cat and threw it into the well.
"Ha! Ha! Ha!" laughed bad old
Humpty Dumpty.

At that moment, the children arrived, racing up the hill. Jack was first, clutching his empty pail, closely followed by Jill.

Jack started to climb the ladder.
"I'm the king of the castle!" cried
Humpty. "Get down, you dirty rascal!"

He kicked the ladder and down it
fell – and down Jack fell with it. Bang!

Jack bumped heads with Jill and they both went tumbling down the hill.

"Ha! Ha! Ha!" laughed bad old Humpty Dumpty.

The king sent the Grand Old Duke of York with his ten thousand men to unseat Humpty Dumpty. They marched up to the top of the hill.

"I'm the king of the castle!" cried Humpty. "Get down you dirty rascals!" He threw stones at the king's men.

"Retreat!" ordered the Duke of York, and they all marched back down the hill again.

"Ha! Ha! Ha!" laughed bad old
Humpty Dumpty.

All that day, Humpty Dumpty sat on
the wall, glorying in his badness.

That night, a short-sighted, high-jumping cow and a little dog were walking up the hill, with a dish and a spoon. The cow and the dog were arguing.

"I can see better than you," said the dog. "I can jump higher than you," said the cow.

"Prove it," said the dog. "Jump over that." He pointed to Humpty Dumpty.

The cow looked at the big round thing. "I can jump over that moon easily," she said.

The cow ran up to the wall and jumped... over Humpty Dumpty.

Humpty was so surprised that he toppled backwards and fell off the wall. Crash! He hit the ground and smashed into pieces.

"Ha! Ha! Ha!" laughed the little dog, while the dish ran away with the spoon.

All the king's horses and all the king's men galloped up, but they couldn't put Humpty together again (though they didn't try very hard).

"He was laughing at us," they said,
"but now the yolk's on him. Ha! ha! ha!"

The king's men caught the runaway dish and spoon.

They used the spoon to scoop Humpty Dumpty into the dish.

Then they took the scrambled egg back to the palace for the king's breakfast. And that was the end of bad old Humpty Dumpty.

START READING is a series of highly enjoyable books for beginner readers. **The books have been carefully graded to match the Book Bands widely used in schools.** This enables readers to be sure they choose books that match their own reading ability.

Look out for the Band colour on the book in our Start Reading logo.

The Bands are:

	Pink Band 1
	Red Band 2
	Yellow Band 3
	Blue Band 4
	Green Band 5
	Orange Band 6
	Turquoise Band 7
	Purple Band 8
	Gold Band 9

START READING books can be read independently or shared with an adult. They promote the enjoyment of reading through satisfying stories supported by fun illustrations.

Alan Durant has written many stories and poems for children of all ages. He loves nursery rhymes and often makes up his own like this one:
I love custard, I love peas / I love macaroni cheese.
I love pickles, I love plums / Put them all inside my tum!

Leah-Ellen Heming once brought back a mouse from her studio in her backpack and cycled it all the way up a very steep hill to her house, where it escaped. The mouse then had a big family, but Leah caught them all and unleashed the mice in her friend's allotment, where they now live happily ever after.